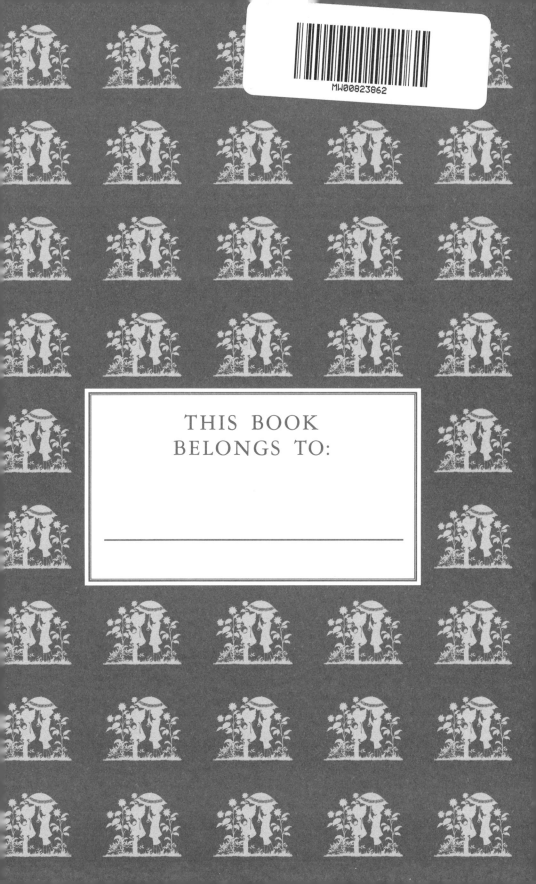

THIS BOOK
BELONGS TO:

_____

WILD
FLOWER
CHILDREN

WILD FLOWER CHILDREN

THE LITTLE PLAYMATES OF THE FAIRIES

ELIZABETH GORDON

ILLUSTRATED BY JANET LAURA SCOTT

DERRYDALE BOOKS
NEW YORK

This 2000 edition is published by Derrydale Books™,
an imprint of Random House Value Publishing, Inc.,
280 Park Avenue, New York, New York 10017.

Derrydale Books™ and design are trademarks of
Random House Value Publishing, Inc.

Random House
New York • Toronto • London • Sydney • Auckland
http://www.randomhouse.com/

Printed and bound in Singapore

Cover design by Sandra Wilentz

ISBN 0-517-16360-8

8 7 6 5 4 3 2 1

This book is lovingly dedicated
to
my wee bit of a Scotch Grandmother,
ELSIE GORDON
and to all others who love
Children and Wild Flowers.

Let's Go Wildflowering

WHAT a difference it would make if there were no wild flowers to call us out into the woods and fields. Why, it is simply not to be imagined; almost as dreary as if there were no babies in the world!

But no matter where you go, across the sands of the desert, or to the tops of the tallest mountain peaks, there are always wild flowers of most delicate beauty growing alone, but not lonely, never drooping or complaining, but brightening their own little spot because God put them there.

In the North, on a railroad trip that I once took in the late May-time, I noticed that the roadsides were painted in a beautiful blending of rose and purple, and I wondered what little artist was doing it.

When the train stopped I went to look, and found that it was a wee little bit of an iris, not much bigger than a four-leaf clover. It was so pretty that it made me very happy and cheerful. I was so happy that a little song sang itself to me—like this:

> Up in the land of the frosts and snows
> A little bit of an iris grows;
> Gaily, over the ground it goes
> Painting the border-lands purple and rose;
> Who ever planted it, nobody knows—
> But up in the land of the frosts and snows
> That little bit of an iris grows—
> That little bit of an iris grows.

One day I happened to tell our publisher man about it; about the dear brave busy little wild flower away off up there doing its bit so nobly, and I asked him if he didn't think, perhaps, that we might have a book of WILD FLOWER CHILDREN.

And he said, "Why, of course we can, and we will!" Now, isn't that just like him, always doing something beautiful for others to enjoy?

So that is why you have this book of the little brothers and sisters of the Flower Children, who live in the woods and the fields and are the little playmates of the fairies.

And the publisher man, and the artist who has made the wonderful pictures, and I, join in wishing you the "splendidest" time with them, and hope that you will love them as much as you have loved your FLOWER CHILDREN and all the other "Nature Children" Books.

I am always your friend,

ELIZABETH GORDON.

HEPATICA
[*Hepatica Triloba*]

Hepatica comes bright and early,
Never tardy, never surly,
Wears a pretty lilac dress
And gives out joy and happiness.

INNOCENCE
[*Houstonia Caerulea*]

Innocence, the pretty thing,
Comes along in early Spring;
Wears sweet slips, the pretty pet,
In dainty shades of violet.

SHOOTING STAR
[Dodecatheon Meadia]
Said Shooting Star, "We're sure and steady,
And come as soon as we are ready;
We're not afraid of April's snows,
That's 'cause we're healthy, I suppose."

WILD FLOWER CHILDREN

PASQUE FLOWER
[Anemone Patens]

Pasque Flower is a prairie child,
Doesn't wait 'till days are mild
But, wrapped in furs, she trips along
Before the Robin sings his song.

DUTCHMAN'S BREECHES
[Dicentra Cucullaria]

The daintiest twins in all the land,
Dutchman's Breeches, hand in hand,
In Springtime tumble down the hill
Just like another Jack and Jill.

SKUNK CABBAGE
[*Symplocarpus Foetidus*]

Skunk Cabbage is a handsome thing
Comes while it is cold in Spring;
Protects his babes from wind and storm
In a big coat that keeps them warm.

WILD FLOWER CHILDREN

JACK IN THE PULPIT
[*Arisaema Triphyllum*]

Each Sunday, on a mossy mound,
The Flower Children gather round
Jack-In-The-Pulpit, while he teaches
Each one, to practice what *he* preaches.

BLUE FLAG
[*Iris Versicolor*]
Blue Flag's as pretty as can be;
Cousin to Mam'selle Fleur De Lis;
Loves cool damp places, and is fond
Of living near a stream or pond.

PAINTED TRILLIUM
[*Trillium Undulatum*]
Said Painted Trillium, "As you see
Our folks observe the rule of three;
The styles may change, but still we cling
To our tri-cornered hats each spring."

WILD FLOWER CHILDREN

YELLOW STAR GRASS
[*Hypoxis Hirsuta*]

Yellow Star Grass hides in play
Among the grasses every day;
But when you call "I spy," she's fair;
Then you can find her anywhere!

SOLOMON'S SEAL
[*Polygonatum Biflorum*]

Solomon's Seal said, looking wise,
"Each may do something if he tries;
I feed the honey bees, the dears,
And keep a record of my years!"

WILD FLOWER CHILDREN

MARSH MARIGOLD
[*Caltha Palustris*]

Marsh Marigold, bright cheerful thing,
Makes glad the days of early Spring;
She sprinkles gold stars one by one
That look like bits chipped from the sun.

MAY APPLE
[*Podophyllien Petaluma*]

In Spring, May Apple, slim and tall,
Carries a pale green parasol;
In Summer time she'll give you fruit,
Unless you're very hard to suit.

PITCHER PLANT
[*Sarracenia Purpurea*]

Said Pitcher Plant, the little elf,
"I fill my cistern for myself;
  And then all sorts of bugs take pains
  To tumble in and clog my drains."

WILD FLOWER CHILDREN

SHOWY LADY'S SLIPPER
[Cypripedium Hirsutum]
Showy Lady's Slipper knows
She's the prettiest thing that grows;
Her Orchid Cousins in the city
Say she's sweet as she is pretty.

WILD FLOWER CHILDREN

SWEET WHITE VIOLET
[Viola Pallens]

Sweet White Violet came to bring
To us the fragrance of the Spring,
Dearest maid in all the wood,
Sweet and modest as she's good.

WILD FLOWER CHILDREN

RED CLOVER
[*Trifolium Pratense*]

Red Clover swaying in the breeze
Holds receptions for the bees;
Doesn't care for sweets himself
But likes to feed each hungry elf.

BUNCH BERRY
[*Cornus Canadensis*]

Bunch Berry wears a gown of white,
And is a dainty woodland sprite;
She comes, the best of little mothers,
To bring her red-clothed Bunch Berry
      brothers.

JEWELWEED
[*Impatiens Biflora*]

"Beware of me," said Jewel Weed,
"I'm very dangerous, indeed;"
 But still the fairies wouldn't stop,
 They teased him just to hear him "pop."

WILD FLOWER CHILDREN

COMMON MALLOW
[*Malva Rotundifolia*]

Little Common Mallow said,
"I could not live inside a bed;
I like to roam just where I please;
The little children play I'm cheese!"

PASTURE ROSE
[*Rosa Humilis*]

Said Pasture Rose, "The Bumble bee
Quite often leaves her babes with me;
I love to hold them next my heart;
I'm sorry when it's time to part!"

WILD FLOWER CHILDREN

DAY FLOWER
[*Commelina Communis*]

Day Flower wears a gown of blue
That only lasts her one day through;
Her mother must be busy quite
To make a new one every night.

ROSE MALLOW
[*Hibiscus Moscheutos*]

Rose Mallow is a happy child,
She likes damp places, in the wild;
Blooms nearly all the summer through
To make a lovely world for you.

WILD FLOWER CHILDREN

GOLD THREAD
[*Ceptis Trifolia*]

Perhaps in woodland walks you've seen
Sir Gold Thread dressed in evergreen;
They say the gnomes and fairies use
His roots of gold to lace their shoes!

MONKEY FLOWER
[*Mimulus Ringens*]

Young Monkey Flower put up a sign;
"Keep Out!   This honey is all mine!"
But Bumble Bee just went ahead,
"I'm sure that don't mean me," he said.

HEAL ALL
[*Prunella Vulgaris*]

Heal All wears a purple bonnet
With some dainty colors on it;
Sometimes brightens her green clothes
With tiny bits of purple bows.

WILD FLOWER CHILDREN

JOB'S TEARS OR, SPIDERWORT
[*Tradescantia Virginiana*]

Job's Tears is such a funny lad!
He weeps all day!   He isn't sad;
Just got the habit!   All the season
He weeps for neither rhyme nor reason.

CATNIP
[Nepeta Cataria]
Old **Dr.** Catnip's glad to call
On pussies big and pussies small;
But says, "If you'll all come to me
I'll make you well without a fee."

ST. JOHN'S WORT
[*Hypericum Perforatum*]

Common St. John's Wort is a tramp,
But he's a jolly little scamp;
Scatters his bloom along the way
Like golden coins his way to pay.

WILD FLOWER CHILDREN

TWIN FLOWER
[*Linnaea Borealis Americana*]

Twin Flower Children, dainty pair,
Sprinkle fragrance on the air;
Seldom, elsewhere will you meet
Flower Children half so sweet.

BELL FLOWER
[*Campanula Rapunculoides*]

Little Bell Flower ran away
From the gardener one fine day,
Never did come back again;
Liked it better on the plain!

WILD FLOWER CHILDREN

STAR-FLOWER
[*Trientalis Americana*]

Dainty Star-Flower seemed to say,
As I raced through the woodland way;
"Don't be afraid, I'll give you light,
Just as the sky-stars do at night!"

WILD FLOWER CHILDREN

BLUE SPRING DAISY
[*Erigeron Pulchellas*]

Blue Spring Daisy said, "I'm chilly
In my lavender gown so frilly
If I try to bloom too soon,
And so I wait till May or June."

COMMON BUTTERCUP
[*Ranunculus Acris*]

Little Common Buttercup,
If you'll hold her gently up
To your dimpled chin, will tell
If you love butter very well.

FALSE LILY OF THE VALLEY
[*Maianthemum Canadense*]

False Lily of the Valley said,
"I'll choose another name instead;
Canada Mayflower it shall be;
There's nothing false, sir, about me."

WILD FLOWER CHILDREN

BELLWORT
]*Uvularia Perfoliata*]
If through the woods you'll walk in May
You'll see the Bellwort children play
At hide and seek, in yellow coats
With their wee cousins, sweet Wild Oats.

DOWNY YELLOW VIOLET
[*Viola Pubescens*]
Downy Yellow Violet said,
"My woodland sister droops her head;
But I go romping on my way,
My face up turned to greet the day."

WILD FLOWER CHILDREN

QUEEN ANNE'S LACE
[*Daucus Carota*]
The fairy babies simply race
Each night to Madame Queen Anne's Lace,
Cuddled so warmly to her breast
She gives each babe a good night's rest.

WILD FLOWER CHILDREN

YELLOW ADDER'S TONGUE
[*Erythronium Americanum*]

By dainty Yellow Adder's Tongue
Such fairy elfin songs are sung
That fairy folk come trooping out
To hear what it is all about!

WILD FLOWER CHILDREN

RHODODENDRON
[*Rhododendron Maximum*]

Rhododendron came to town
In her green and rose pink gown;
She's so pretty that we give
Her the nicest spots to live.

LAMB-KILL
[*Kalmia Augustifolia*]

Lamb-Kill's as pretty as can be;
He can't be trusted though, you see,
He's mischievous, and feeds the sheep
Some sort of stuff that makes them sleep.

WILD FLOWER CHILDREN

CANADA LILY
[Lilium Canadense]

Canada Lily grows quite wild
But she's a gentle graceful child,
She loves the meadows where she plays
Happily through the summer days.

CREAM-CUP
[Platystemon Californica]

Cream-Cup comes, the pretty thing,
To gladden California's Spring,
You'll meet them everywhere in flocks
Clambering over hills and rocks.

BABY BLUE EYES
[*Nemophila Insignis*]
Baby Blue Eyes comes in Spring
Dainty dimpled smiling thing;
Calls to us from far away,
"Won't you please come out to play?"

WILD FLOWER CHILDREN

CALIFORNIA LARKSPUR
[*Delphinium Americanum*]
California Larkspur plays
With Golden Poppies all his days,
Prettiest children ever seen
Dressed in gold and blue and green.

WILD FLOWER CHILDREN

WILD MORNING GLORY
[Convolulus Sepium]

Wild Morning Glory runs away
Along the woodland paths to play;
She climbs about with easy grace
And hangs her bright bells every place.

WILD FLOWER CHILDREN

CARDINAL FLOWER
[Lobelia Cardinalis]

Stately Madame Cardinal Flower
Holds receptions by the hour;
Invites those whom she likes the best,
And Humming Bird's her favorite guest.

TURKS CAP LILY
[*Lilium Superbum*]
Said Turks Cap Lily, "As you see
I'm as industrious as can be;
That's why I'm rich, and can afford
To give such swarms of bees their board."

WILD COLUMBINE
[*Aquilegia Canadensis*]

"I keep my sweets," said Columbine,
"For Humming Bird, a friend of mine;
   He comes at sun-down every night,
   And is *so* grateful and polite."

WILD FLOWER CHILDREN

WHITE CLOVER
[*Trifolium Repens*]

The Robin heard white Clover say,
"When I'm grown I'll be Sweet Hay,
To feed the cow so she can give
Nice milk to help wee children live."

EVENING PRIMROSE
[*Onogra Biennis*]

Said Evening Primrose, "I wake up,
When twilight comes, and fill my cup
With sweetest honey for my friends
The moths, who come when day-time ends.

WILD FLOWER CHILDREN

WILD GERANIUM OR CRANESBILL
[*Geranium Maculatum*]

Along the wooded roads I grow
And children pluck me as they go,
And say my flowers are sweet and gay,
Which makes me happy all the day.

WILD FLOWER CHILDREN

FIREWEED
[*Epilobium Augustifolium*]

When fire fiends through the woodland race
Leaving a blackened barren place,
Then Fire Weed knows that it's his duty
To make the burned land bloom with beauty.

LUPINE
[Lupinus Perrenis]

In sand dunes hot or meadows **gay**
The little Lupines love to play;
In dainty gowns of violet blue
They'll nod a glad "Good-day" to **you.**

WILD FLOWER CHILDREN

PEARLY EVERLASTING
[*Anaphalis Margaritacea*]

Around the hillsides in the sun
The Pearly Everlastings run;
Never find enough to eat
But still they're plump and clean and neat.

WATER LILY
[Castalia Adorato]
Water Lily is a queen,
Wears sweet robes of white and green;
Sleeps so sweetly all night long,
Lulled by Green Frog's slumber song.

YELLOW POND LILY
[Nymphaea Advena]

Yellow Pond Lily laughed and said,
"Some one splashed water on my head;"
Said Spotted Trout, "Perhaps t'was I
When I jumped out to catch a fly."

65

WATER ARUM
[Calla Palustris]

Water Arum shares his bog
With his good neighbor Mr. Frog;
Dressed in his best, when day time ends
The Frog's grand concert he attends.

WILD FLOWER CHILDREN

SKULL CAP
[*Scutellaria Integrifolia*]
Skull Cap keeps a hat shop; he
Is just as busy as can be;
That's where the fairies, cunning chaps,
Get all their pointed tasseled caps.

BULL THISTLE
[*Cirsium Lanceolatum*]
Bull Thistle waves a thousand lances
So bugs and beetles take no chances;
But butterflies and honey bees
Are welcome any time they please.

WILD FLOWER CHILDREN

COMMON MULLEIN
[*Verbascum Thapsus*]

Common Mullein's lots of fun,
He loves the children every one;
His velvet leaves when torn he'll lend
To any fairy who will mend.

BROAD LEAVED ARROW HEAD
[*Sagittaria Latifolia*]
Lovely Broad Leaved Arrow Head
Lives in Madame River's bed;
Loves to wade and splash all day
And with the Minnow children play.

LARGE PURPLE ORCHIS
[Habenaria Fimbriata]

Large Purple Orchis loves to grow
Where crowds of people do not go;
But you're quite welcome, if you'll tramp
To where she lives (It's rather damp).

WILD FLOWER CHILDREN

BUTTER AND EGGS
[*Linaria Vulgaris*]

Said Butter and Eggs, "We can afford
To give Sir Bumble Bee his board;
But when he's gone we close the door
Or we'd have Ants in by the score!"

WILD FLOWER CHILDREN

INDIAN PAINT BRUSH
[*Castilleja Coccinea*]

Indian Paint Brush holds his cup
Of brilliant scarlet petals up;
That's all he does; for he's a shirk
And lives on other people's work.

BLACK EYED SUSAN
[*Rudbeckia Hirta*]

Saucy Little Black-Eyed Susan
When her mother caught her snoozin',
Rubbed her sleepy eyes and said,
"Guess I'll toddle off to bed."

WILD FLOWER CHILDREN

MOSS PINK
[*Phlox Subulata*]

Little Moss Pink creeps around
All summer on the sandy ground;
Daintiest creature ever seen
In her gown of pink and green.

WILD FLOWER CHILDREN

CAT-TAIL
[*Typha Latifolia*]

The Cat-Tail people roam around
Through any sort of marshy ground;
If you'll go by their house at night
You'll see their yellow candle light.

COMMON PLANTAIN
[*Plantago Major*]

Common Plantain thought he'd play
Around the house·one summer day;
Gardener called him "Naughty Weed!"
Which made him very sad indeed!

WILD FLOWER CHILDREN

COMMON MILK WEED
[*Asclepias Syrica*]

Said Common Milk Weed, "When I've fed
The bees, I put my babes to bed
In silken cradles, where they sway
Rocked by the little Winds all day.

WILD FLOWER CHILDREN

LADY'S SORREL
[Oxalis Cornucalate]

Lady's Sorrel sleeps so tight
Throughout the peaceful summer night;
But her eyes fly open wide
When Sunbeam frolics by her side!

DOWNY PHLOX
[*Phlox Pilosa*]

Said Downy Phlox, "Of all the West,
I love the rolling prairies best;"
Cousin Sweet William smiled and said,
"I like my own soft garden bed."

SHOWY GOLDEN ROD
[*Solidago Speciosa*]

"Our family is so large you see,"
Said Showy Golden Rod to me,
"It keeps me nodding all the day
To cousins who go by this way!"

NEW ENGLAND ASTER
[*Aster Nova-Anglae*]

New England Aster said, "Dear me!
I've been as lazy as can be;"
So dressed in purple, off she flew
And traveled all the country through.

SMOOTH ASTER
[*Aster Laevis*]
Wild Smooth Aster loves to play
Along the roadside every day;
Waving her banner blue in glee,
Perhaps to you, perhaps to me.

WILD FLOWER CHILDREN

DOWNY GENTIAN
[Gentiana Puberula]

Downy Gentian rings his bell
His friends the butterflies to tell
It's honey time; and how they all
Come trooping when they hear his call.

CLOSED GENTIAN
[*Gentiana Andrewsii*]

"O Bottle Gentian," begged the bees
"Open and give us honey, please?"
  But Bottle Gentian shook his head,
"Belongs to Bumble Bee," he said.

WILD FLOWER CHILDREN

HEART LEAVED ASTER
[*Aster Cordifolius*]

"I wear my heart outside, you know,"
Said Heart Leaved Aster, "That is so
The bird, the butterfly, the bee
May tell their secrets all to me."

SILVER ROD
[*Solidago Bicolor*]

Said Silver Rod, "My cousins all
Wear robes of gold the livelong Fall;
It's unbecoming to me quite,
And so I dress in creamy white.

VIRGIN'S BOWER
[Clematis Verticillaris]

Said Virgin's Bower, "I spend my time
Teaching the younger ones to climb;
But when Fall comes we all look weird,
For then folks call us, 'Old Man's Beard.'"

GROUND IVY
[*Nepeta Hederacea*]

Ground Ivy, "Gill-Run-Over-The-Ground,"
Scatters her purple flowers around;
She says she dearly loves to stay
Where little children romp and play.

CLINTONIA
[*Clintonia Borealis*]

Clintonia borrowed with a smile
Cousin Lily-Of-The-Valley's style;
The gown became her very well
Trimmed with her own sweet yellow bell.

FROSTWEED
[*Helianthemum Canadense*]

Frostweed's sometimes called Rock Rose,
He doesn't mind how cold it grows;
Laughs, and thinks it's rather nice
To trim his cap with bits of ice.

THOROUGH-WORT
[*Rupatorium Perfoliatum*]

Said Thorough-Wort, "I used to be
Gathered to make a bitter tea;
So, I'm disliked, but I'll outlive it,
Now folks know better than to give it."